the

Didi Dodo FUTURE SPY

series

the

series

By TOM ANGLEBERGER

Illustrated by

JARED CHAPMAN

Didi Dodo
#2
FUTURE SPY
Robo-Dodo Rumble

ROBO-DODO COOKIES

Amulet Books · New York

Cataloging-in-Publication Data has been applied for and may be obtained from the Library of Congress.

ISBN 978-1-4197-3688-9

Text copyright © 2019 Tom Angleberger
Illustrations copyright © 2019 Jared Chapman
Book design by Steph Stilwell

Printed and bound in U.S.A.
10 9 8 7 6 5 4 3 2 1

Amulet Books are available at special discounts when purchased in quantity for premiums and promotions as well as fundraising or educational use. Special editions can also be created to specification. For details, contact specialsales@abramsbooks.com or the address below.

Amulet Books® is a registered trademark of Harry N. Abrams, Inc.

ABRAMS The Art of Books
195 Broadway, New York, NY 10007
abramsbooks.com

To Cynthia Leitich Smith
—T. A.

CONTENTS

Opening

My phone rang.

"Hello, this is Koko Dodo's Cookie Shop. Koko Dodo speaking! What are you telling me?" I said.

"How-dee, neigh-bor," said a robot voice. "Would you like to—"

"Wait just a minute!" I interrupted. "Is this one of those robocalls?"

"What is a ro-bo-call?" asked the robot voice.

"You know! One of those awful calls where you answer the phone and all you hear is a recording and the recording wants to sell you something."

"This is not a re-cor-ding," said the robot voice.

"But you sound a lot like a robot!"

"I AM a ro-bot."

"Oh, well that explains it," I said. "Sorry if I was rude. I just hate those calls that try to sell you something. So . . . What do you want?"

"I want to sell you some-thing," said the robot. "I am sell-ing coo-kies."

"Cookies? What are you telling me about cookies? I am Koko Dodo! I bake my own cookies in my own cookie shop! Of course I do not want to buy any cookies!"

"O-kay, I will find some-one else to buy my coo-kies. Good-bye, neigh-bor."

The robot hung up.

I went back to baking my own cookies, but I kept wondering: Why did the robot keep calling me "neighbor"?

PART 1

The Price
Is Wrong

Chapter 1

t was a slow morning at the cookie shop.

I had been baking for hours with my helper, the Queen. We had made many, many cookies.

But we did not have many, many customers.

In fact, we did not have ANY customers.

"Where are all the customers, Your Majesty?" I asked.

"I don't know, Koko," said the Queen. "Even the three baby chicks haven't been here!"

"Well, at least we won't have to clean the baby chick poop off the chairs today," I said. "But what are we going to do with all these uneaten cookies? I'll go out of business this way!"

"Wait," said the Queen. "Someone's coming!"

I opened the door.

"Hello and welcome to—"

"Look out!" said Didi Dodo, who was the someone who was coming. And boy was she coming fast!

She zoomed through the door on her

roller skates and crashed into the counter. Unsold cookies went everywhere!

The Queen was hit on the head by a double-chocolate chunk cookie! She would have been knocked out if her cardboard crown hadn't protected her.

"Sorry about the cookies," said Didi Dodo.

SLAM

"Don't be worrying about it!" I said. "No one was buying them. You're the first customer we've had all day!"

"Sorry, Koko," said Didi. "I didn't come to buy cookies. I came because . . ."

Didi Dodo sprang to her feet—actually, to her wheels—and waved one wing in the air.

She held her beak high.

Her eyes sparkled.

"I, Didi Dodo, Future Spy, have a daring plan!" she shouted.

"I need customers, not a daring plan!"

"But my daring plan is to get your customers back!"

"Get them back from where?" I asked.

"From there!" she said and pointed her wing out the window and across the street.

Chapter 2

I looked out the window and saw a giant dodo across the street!

"There's a giant dodo across the street!" I yelled.

"No," said Didi Dodo. "There's a giant Robo-Dodo across the street!"

"What are you telling me about a Robo-Dodo?" I yelled. "What is a Robo-Dodo?"

"A Robo-Dodo is a very large robot that is shaped like a dodo and sells cheap cookies."

"CHEAP COOKIES?!" I screamed. "No wonder I lost all my customers! How cheap are they?"

Just then, an elephant wearing a top hat ran past the store. His mouth was full, and cookie crumbs were falling out.

Didi opened the door and said, "Excuse me, how much did those cookies cost?"

"A penny," said the elephant wearing a top hat.

"COOKIES FOR A PENNY EACH?!" I yelled.

"No," said the elephant. "All the cookies you can eat for one penny!"

"ALL THE COOKIES YOU CAN EAT FOR ONE PENNY?! I AM RUINED! I WILL HAVE TO CLOSE MY SHOP!"

"Just a second!" demanded the Queen. "How do the cookies taste?"

"Oh, they're terrible," said the elephant. "Like chewing moldy bricks."

"What are you telling me with the moldy bricks?" I asked. "Wouldn't you rather have one of my delicious, fresh peanut butter yumyums?"

"How much?" asked the elephant.

"Only $1.59," I said.

"What a rip-off!" yelled the elephant. "I can eat robot cookies for 159 days for that much! Now, if you'll excuse me, I'm going back for more!"

The elephant stampeded across the street.

"Didi Dodo," I said.

"Yes, Koko Dodo?" she said, her eye already sparkling.

"I need a daring plan."

"I have one!" she shouted.

Chapter 3

T he first part of my plan," said Didi, "is for you to open this present I got you for National Cookie Day."

She handed me a crumpled and smooshed present.

"Wow! Thanks!" I said. "But National Cookie Day isn't until tomorrow. Should I wait?"

"No," said Didi. "You're going to need them right away."

I opened the box. It was a pair of roller skates! Just like the ones Didi always wears.

"Put them on!" she said.

"I do love to skate," I said. "But this hardly seems like the right time to go to the roller rink!"

"We're not going to the roller rink," Didi replied. "We're going to Gertrude's Used Ski Jumps."

"What are you telling me about a ski jump?"

"All part of my Daring Plan," said Didi.

"Any plan that involves roller skates AND a ski jump is TOO DARING! Don't you have a not-so-daring plan?"

"Well," she said, "you could get a paint-brush and start painting a big GOING OUT OF BUSINESS sign."

I laced up my new roller skates.

We skated down the street to Gertrude's Used Ski Jumps.

"Hey, Gertrude," said Didi, "do you mind if we use the big jump?"

"Help yourself," said Gertrude. "I've got to go." She ran past us with a penny clinched in her hoof!

We took an elevator to the top of the biggest ski jump.

"I don't like elevators, heights, or ski jumps," I said. "I've changed my mind."

"Too late," said Didi.

She grabbed my hand and pulled me over the edge of the ramp.

Interlude

We landed on top of the Robo-Dodo.

Well, actually, I landed on top of the Robo-Dodo. Didi Dodo landed on top of me.

"Yowch!" I said.

"Sorry," said Didi Dodo.

"Hi!" said the three baby chicks.

"Three baby chicks," I said. "What on earth are you doing way up here?"

"Pooping," said the three baby chicks.

"What are you telling me with the pooping?" I asked. "Why would you do that up here?"

"It's a natural part of the digestive system," said the first chick.

"But why would you do that up here?" Didi asked.

"We couldn't find any chairs, so we thought we'd poop on top of this statue," said the second chick.

"Birds love to poop on statues," said the third chick.

"But this isn't a statue! It's a robot that makes cookies," explained Didi Dodo.

"Uh-oh," said the chicks. "I hope the robot doesn't get mad at us for pooping on it."

Just then, the huge head of the Robo-Dodo turned toward us.

Its eyes lit up.

"Uh-oh," said the chicks. "It's mad at us."

BZZRAP!

The eyes shot lasers at us!

We all jumped! The lasers hit the spot where we had been standing! And then the spot where we had been standing was just a big hole!

"We've got to get off this Robo-Dodo!" I yelled.

"Not according to my daring plan," said Didi Dodo.

Her eyes started to light up. But so did the Robo-Dodo's!

"It's going to fire again!" I yelled. "Just go ahead and tell us the daring plan already!"

"We need to get IN this Robo-Dodo!"

And she jumped into the hole!

I heard the Robo-Dodo go *BZZRAP* again, so I grabbed the three baby chicks and jumped in after her.

PART 2

Interview with a Robo-Dodo

Chapter 4

We fell down through the hole into the insides of the Robo-Dodo and landed in something smelly and smooshy.

"Uh-oh," said the chicks.

"We've landed in a giant bowl of instant cookie mix!" I yelled.

"This is where the Robo-Dodo makes its cookies!" Didi yelled back.

"We want to eat cookies," said the chicks. "Not BE cookies! Get us out of here!"

Didi and I tried, but the walls of the giant bowl were too slippery and too steep.

"I hope you have a daring plan to get us out before the Robo-Dodo adds the eggs and butter," I told Didi.

She held her beak up high, she waved her wing, she—

"Too late!" squawked the baby chicks.

Giant hoses started spraying us with raw eggs and melted butter.

"This is disgusting," said Didi.

"I'll say," I said. "These are NOT fresh ingredients! It's no wonder the cookies taste so bad!"

"The cookies are going to taste like US if we don't get out of here," said Didi. "Look!"

I was afraid to look, so I closed my eyes.

But I couldn't close my ears.

I heard a scary metal whirring sound!

It could only be one thing . . . a giant robo-mixer!

"Is it a giant robo-mixer?"

"Yes!" said the baby chicks.

"Does it have big scary mixing blades?"

"Yes!" said the baby chicks.

"Are we going to get chopped up into little pieces?"

"Yes!" said the baby chicks.

"NO!" said Didi Dodo. "Because I have a daring plan!"

She lifted her beak, waved her wing, made her eyes sparkle, and then jumped over the blade and grabbed on to the metal thingy that the blades are on. You know, the straight part that connects to the motor and goes around really really really fast? That part.

"Hurry, Koko!" yelled Didi, who was now spinning around really really really fast, too.

"Hold on, baby chicks!" I yelled, and I flapped, floundered, and flung myself over the blade just in time.

I tried to grab on to the metal thingy, but I missed and grabbed on to one of Didi's roller skates instead.

"Hold on, Koko!"

"What are you telling me with the hold on! Of course I am holding on!" I shouted, spinning around really really really fast.

"Good," she yelled, "because I am going to let go!"

"What are you telling me with the— AAAAAAAAAAAAH!"

Chapter 5

When Didi let go, we were all flung out of the bowl.

"AAAAAAH!"

We all screamed. When we saw where we were headed, we kept screaming and got louder!

"AAAAAAAAAAAH!"

We were headed for a conveyor belt that was moving thousands and thousands of cookies through a really long oven!

"Oh no!" yelled the baby chicks.

"We're going to get baked!" I yelled.

"Not if we speed skate!" yelled Didi.

I had to do a double somersault with a twist in midair, but I was able to land on my wheels.

Didi was able to land on me.

The chicks were squished in between.

I zigged and zagged to dodge all the cookies and zoomed right through the oven and out the other side.

All the cookies went down into a big funnel, but I jumped over that, and we landed near some computers and filing cabinets.

We were toasted, but not roasted.

"That plan was not just daring; it was charring!" I said.

"But it worked!" said Didi. "The oven even burned off all that gooey raw egg and butter."

"Yes, it was a ver-y good plan," said a robot voice. "But I have a bet-ter one."

"Uh-oh," said the baby chicks.

"Who said that?" gasped Didi.

"We did," said the baby chicks.

"No, I meant the part before that."

"That was me," said a robot voice.

"Who are you?" demanded Didi.

"I am the e-lec-tric brain of Ro-bo Do-do," said Robo-Dodo through a speaker. "Who are you?"

"I am Didi Dodo, Future Spy!"

"Does that mean you are from the fu-ture?" asked the electric brain. "Or does it mean you have lots of fu-tur-is-tic gadg-ets and spy gear?"

"No, it means that I will be a spy some-day in the future."

"O-K," said Robo-Dodo. "And who are the small birds poo-ping on my stuff?"

"Those are the baby chicks," I said.

"And who are you?" asked Robo-Dodo.

"I am Koko Dodo!"

"Oh, you are the one I want to put out of biz-ness."

And then it did a robot laugh.

"Ha . . . Ha . . . Ha . . . Ha . . ."

Chapter 6

was mad!

"What are you telling me? Do you mean you're ruining my business on purpose?"

"Of course! I am a ro-bot. We on-ly do things on pur-pose."

"But why are you doing it?"

"That part of my plan is a se-cret!"

And then it did another robot laugh.

"Ha . . . Ha . . . Ha . . . Ha . . ."

Now I was REALLY mad!

I started yelling. I wanted to yell some bad words, but I don't know any. So I made some up.

HOOBER ROOFUS! MEEGA WEEGA DIMPLEHAM!!

"Those words are not in my da-ta-bank," said Robo-Dodo. "Give me a second to add them."

"Uh . . . OK," I said.

"Pssst," whispered Didi. She waved her wing just a little. She raised her beak just a little. Her eyes sparkled just a little.

I knew she had a daring plan, but I didn't want Robo-Dodo to know she had a daring plan.

"You are right," she told Robo-Dodo. "Your secret plan is much better than my daring plan. So, we'll just go now, OK?"

"Uh . . . OK . . ." said Robo-Dodo.

Didi started to skate back the way we had come.

"No! Not that way!" said Robo-Dodo. "Use the mee-ga wee-ga door!"

A robo-hand pointed to a door marked EXIT.

The chicks jumped on my back. We skated through the door and came out of Robo-Dodo's . . . uh . . . well, I think I better just say "exit," OK? OK? Enough! Mind your own business!

Didi and I climbed down Robo-Dodo's metal tail feathers and ended in the street in front of my store. There were cookie customers everywhere . . . except in my store! They were all standing in line to buy Robo-Dodo's cookies!

"Why did we just leave?" I asked Didi. "I thought you were going to find out what Robo-Dodo's secret plan was?"

"I did!" shouted Didi. "While you were yelling at it, I found this in a filing cabinet."

She held up a sheet of paper that said:

Robo-Dodo's Secret Plan

1. Find a cookie store.

2. Move in next door and sell cookies for much less.

3. Steal all the customers.

Hey, look!

CHEAP COOKIES

4. Wait for first store to go out of business.

5. Sell cookies for much, much more! Ha . . . Ha . . . Ha . . .

Interlude

The worst part of it all was that Robo-Dodo's plan was working!

"Look, Didi, the line of customers is so long that nobody could get into my store even if they wanted to."

"Trust me," grumbled a cactus on a pogo stick, "we don't want to! Your cookies are too expensive!"

"But I make them from scratch every day with my own two wings!"

"Face it, chump," said the cactus, "you're too slow and old-fashioned."

"But—" I started, but I was interrupted by screeching tires!

The cactus pogo-sticked out of the way just as a fancy limo skidded to a stop.

A horse got out. It was the President of the United States of America, Horse G. Horse.

"Get out of my way!" he yelled and shoved us aside.

"Look out, President of the United States coming through! I'm the President, so I get to cut the line! Outta my way! I want cheap cookies and I want them now!"

Lots of my other old customers were in line, too. I saw Mimi Kiwi, Vanessa Cow Cow, twenty-three pig scientists, Leggy Snake, Debra Zebra, and . . . Inspector Flytrap and Nina!

"Inspector Flytrap! What are you telling me? Are you buying cookies from that robot, too?"

"No way, Koko," said Inspector Flytrap. "We only buy cookies from you!"

"Oh, thank goodness!" I said. "Are you here to buy cookies right now?"

"Sorry, Koko. We're on our way to solve a BIG DEAL mystery down at the harbor. Something strange is in the water."

He and Nina pushed through the crowd and zoomed off toward the harbor on their skateboard.

"Even Nina wouldn't eat my cookies..." I sobbed.

"But she did chew a hole in the President's tire," said Didi.

"Well, that's good news!"

"Also, I have a daring plan!"

"That's GREAT news!"

PART 3

The Monster from Beneath the Sea

Chapter 7

ome on in the store and have a cookie—a GOOD cookie—and tell me your plan," I said.

"Can we come, too?" asked the baby chicks.

"Yes, but no pooping on the chairs," I said.

"We promise," lied the baby chicks.

We all went into the store.

"I just pulled the last batch of cookies out of the oven," the Queen said.

"Thank you, Your Majesty," I said. "I just hope it is not the last batch EVER! We could be out of business by lunchtime."

"Don't worry," said Didi with her eyes sparkling. "It's going to be Robo-Dodo's last batch when we use my daring plan!"

"Whoo-hoo!" said the baby chicks.

"We are going to sneak back into Robo-Dodo and switch all the ingredients tubes," said Didi, her beak in the air.

"Yee-haw!" said the baby chicks.

"And the robot's last batch will be EXPLODING COOKIES!" yelled Didi, waving her wing in the air.

"Yahooooo!" shouted the baby chicks, waving their wings in the air!

"Hold on just a dimpleham minute!" I said, waving my wing in the air. "What are you telling me with the exploding cookies?"

"You know . . . vinegar and baking soda? You put them together and they explode?"

"Of course I know that," I said. "That's why I would never put vinegar and baking soda into the same recipe! It would make a big mess in my kitchen!"

"Exactly!" said Didi. "And you only make small batches. Robo-Dodo makes BIG batches! Just imagine what would happen if it filled that giant bowl of cookie mix with vinegar and baking soda . . . KABLOOEY!"

"Yippie-I-O-Ki-Yay!" yelled the baby chicks.

"I'm sorry, Didi," I said. "We cannot do that."

"What?" asked Didi.

"Why not?" quacked the Queen.

"Aw, come on, please," begged the baby chicks. "We want to see Robo-Dodo blow up!"

"I'm sorry," I said. "But I am a cookie baker. I bake things and I make things, but I don't blow things up."

Chapter 8

A single tear rolled down the Queen's bill.

"Koko Dodo, your speech has moved me to tears!" she said royally.

"Yes," said Didi Dodo. "It reminded us all to be kind and good."

"NO!" declared the Queen. "It reminded me that I'll be out of a job if he has to close this cookie shop! I decree that you stop squawking and do something!"

"But what can we do?" I moaned. "Look out the window! Look at all those customers lined up for Robo-Dodo's cheap cookies!"

"They're gone," said the baby chicks.

"What are you telling me with gone?" I gasped.

"Yep," said the baby chicks. "They all ran off screaming while you guys were squawking and we were pooping on the chairs."

We ran outside to see.

The chicks were right! Everybody was gone. We were standing in the middle of an empty street!

Actually, it wasn't totally empty.

Inspector Flytrap and Nina were zooming toward us on their skateboard.

"Aha!" Flytrap was yelling. "I have solved the BIG DEAL mystery at the harbor! The strange thing in the water was a GIANT SEA MONSTER that's going to EAT the whole CITY!"

"Big eel," said Nina, pointing straight up with her hoof as they whizzed past us.

We looked up and saw the head of a giant sea monster rising above the city.

"Uh-oh," said the baby chicks.

"That IS a big eel!" I shouted. "What should we do now?"

"Get out of my way!" yelled a rude voice. It was President Horse G. Horse galloping away from the monster.

"Mr. President, shouldn't you do something about the eel?"

"I AM doing something! I'm getting the hoober rufus out of here!" he neighed and galloped off.

"What should we do now?" I shouted.

A motor roared. Tires screeched. A food truck skidded to a stop.

"Hop in!" shouted Penguini, who was driving the food truck. "I'll give you all a ride out of town! And free breadsticks."

"No, thanks," said Didi.

"What are you telling me with the 'no thanks'?" I squawked. "Don't you want to get away from the sea monster?"

Didi raised her beak in the air.

"Uh-oh," said the chicks.

Didi waved her wing.

"Uh-oh," said the Queen.

Didi looked at me with her eyes sparkling.

"Uh-oh," I said.

I turned to Penguini.

"No, thanks," I said. "Didi has a daring plan to save the city, so we'll stay here."

"But we will take some free breadsticks," said the baby chicks.

Penguini tossed the breadsticks out the window and zoomed off.

We were alone in the city with a giant sea monster that was now taking big bites out of buildings!

"What do we do now?" I asked.

"First," said Didi, still waving her wing, "we get a penny!"

Chapter 9

We got the penny. That was all the money that was left in my store, since no one had bought any cookies all day!

"Now what do we do with the penny?" I asked.

"We're going to buy cookies from Robo-Dodo," said Didi Dodo.

"WHAT ARE YOU TELLING US?!" we all yelled.

"I'm telling you that we are going to buy cookies from Robo-Dodo," said Didi Dodo.

"But we don't want its nasty cookies," said the baby chicks. "Yuk!"

"And I don't want to support its business," I said.

"And I was going to use that penny to get a gumball," said the Queen.

"Don't you trust me?" asked Didi Dodo.

"Of course we do," I said.

"Then tighten up your skates, 'cause we've got another jump to make!"

"What do we do?" asked the chicks.

"Do you know any musical numbers?"

"We learned to sing 'Achy Breaky Heart' and do the Achy Breaky country line dance by watching YouTube."

"Great," Didi told them. "Just wait for your cue."

Minutes later, we were up at the top of Gertrude's Used Ski Jump ramp again. The giant eel monster was right in front of it.

"This ramp is even scarier now," I cried, "because there's a giant eel monster right in front of it!"

"You'll just have to make sure you jump over the giant eel monster!" said Didi Dodo, and she pushed me over the edge.

SHOVE!

We zoomed down the ramp, then up the ramp, then through the air . . . directly at the giant eel's giant mouth!

I may be a flightless bird, but I was flapping my wings like crazy!

But as I went higher and higher, the eel opened its mouth wider and wider!

"We're not going to make it!" I yelled to Didi.

"Yes . . . we . . . are . . ." said Didi, also flapping like crazy. "Baby chicks, hit it!"

Far down below, the baby chicks began to sing "Achy Breaky Heart" and do the Achy Breaky country line dance.

The eel couldn't help itself. It glanced down to see who was singing and dancing.

It was just enough!

We barely cleared its huge mouth, then skated up its head, past its beady eyes, onto its fin, and jumped into the air again.

Down below, the chicks were yelling "Yee-haw" and waving tiny bandanas.

We landed back on top of Robo-Dodo, dodged a few laser blasts, and skated straight into the same hole we had used earlier.

But this time, Didi grabbed on to the butter hose and I grabbed on to Didi. She swung us out of the bowl, over the oven, and right into Robo-Dodo's control room.

"Boo-hoo-hoo," said Robo-Dodo. "All my cus-to-mers have gone a-way."

"Don't worry," said Didi, holding up the penny. "We found one more customer for you."

"Great," said Robo-Dodo. "Which one of you wants all the coo-kies you can eat?"

"Oh, it's not for us," said Didi. "It's for the giant eel."

"Uh . . ." said Robo-Dodo. "How ma-ny coo-kies can a gi-ant eel eat?"

"TONS!" said Didi. "So you better start baking."

"I do not want to," said Robo-Dodo. "That sounds like a bad biz-ness deal for me."

"Too bad," said Didi. "You're a robot. You have to do what you are programmed to do, and you are programmed to give your customers all the cookies they can eat in return for . . . one penny."

Didi put the penny into Robo-Dodo's coin slot.

"Nooooooooooooooooooooooo," groaned Robo-Dodo as the penny clanked down into its money box.

A little screen flashed PAID.

"Oh well," said Robo-Dodo. "I guess a do-do's got-ta do what a do-do's got-ta do. But I do not like it!"

Just then, my phone rang.

"This is Koko Dodo," I said. "What are you telling me?"

"Koko, this is the Queen! The giant eel monster is headed downtown to destroy famous city landmarks!"

"Oh no!" I yelled. "The Queen says the giant eel monster is headed downtown to destroy famous city landmarks!"

"Ask her to follow it on her motor scooter," said Didi. "We'll be there as soon as we can!"

"But, Didi," I said, "how can we get the cookies to the eel if—"

But Didi was already waving her wing, lifting her beak, and doing the sparkly eye thing.

"I have a plan!"

"How daring is it?" I asked.

"How dar-ing is it?" Robo-Dodo asked.

Didi flipped a switch that said MANUAL LEG CONTROLS.

"Hold on to your beaks," she said, "we're about to find out!"

That's a Lot of Cookies

Chapter 10

idi pulled a huge lever. Robo-Dodo took a giant step forward with its right leg.

STOMP! The whole city seemed to shake!

She pulled another lever, and it took another giant step with its left leg.

STOMP!

"Hey!" yelled Didi, pushing and pulling the levers faster and faster. "This actually works!"

STOMP STOMP STOMP STOMP!

I looked out of one of Robo-Dodo's eyes. We were about to stomp on . . . MY COOKIE SHOP!

"Look out!" I yelled.

"Don't worry about me," ordered Didi, spinning a steering wheel so that Robo-Dodo just missed stepping on my shop. "I need you to reprogram Robo-Dodo's recipe."

"What are you telling me?"

"I'm telling you that its cookies are terrible."

"That is hurt-ful," said Robo-Dodo, "but al-so true. I wish I could bake like you do, Ko-ko. Boo-hoo-hoo . . ."

"Aw," I said. "That's so sweet."

"Would you two cut the yakkity yakkity and fix that recipe?!" yelled Didi. "We've got to make sure these cookies are the best-tasting thing in the whole city!"

I started typing my best recipe into Robo-Dodo's electronic brain. Let me tell you, it is not so easy to type while riding in a giant metal bird that is running down the street on robot legs and crashing into every trash can and medium-size taco stand in sight.

Finally, I fixed all the typos and hit Save.

Then I hit Bake.

Koko Dodo and Robo-Dodo's Chocolate Fish and Chip Cookies

This recipe makes approximately 58,392 cookies.

YOU WILL NEED:

- 82 50-gallon tanks of Robo-Dodo Brand™ instant cookie mix
- 3 50-gallon tanks of Robo-Dodo Brand™ fake butter
- 2 tons of Robo-Dodo Brand™ Almost Chocolate™ chocolatey chips
- 257 boxes of baking soda
- One boatload of fresh-caught fish
- Pinch of salt
- A giant cookie-making robot

DIRECTIONS:

1. Tell giant cookie-making robot to make the cookies.
2. Enjoy!

ALTERNATE RECIPE TO MAKE JUST ONE COOKIE

YOU WILL NEED:

- 1 packet of Betty Crocker Mug Treats Soft-Baked Chocolate Chip Cookie Mix
- 1 can of tuna
- 1 microwave-safe coffee mug
- A microwave oven
- A can opener if needed for tuna
- Measuring spoon (teaspoon)

DIRECTIONS:

1. Tear open one packet of mug cookie mix. Pour the mix into mug.

2. Open can of tuna carefully so that the juice does not spill out.

3. This step should probably be done over the sink or at least a paper towel. If tuna juice goes everywhere, your kitchen is going to stink!

4. Carefully pour tuna juice from can into teaspoon. Then pour tuna juice from teaspoon into can. Do this four times. (Five times if you spilled some.)

5. Save the tuna for your lunch.

6. Use the spoon to stir the juice into the mix until it's all nice and gloopy. Use the spoon to push all the gloop into the bottom of the mug.

7. Place mug in microwave. Close the door. Microwave for sixty seconds.

8. LET IT COOL DOWN!!! ARE YOU CRAZY, GRABBING A HOT CUP AND SPOONING OUT MOLTEN HOT FISH COOKIE?!

9. Enjoy!

Chapter 11

Robo-Dodo fired up its ovens and started squirting ingredients into the mixing bowl.

"The first batch will be rea-dy in twelve min-utes," it said.

"Great!" hollered Didi. "Now we just need to catch that eel!"

My phone rang.

"This is—"

"I know who it is!" quacked the Queen. "You dodos better get down here fast! The eel just busted up the central library!"

"That does it!" yelled Didi Dodo. "I'm putting this thing on turbo speed!"

She pushed a big button that read WARNING: DO NOT PUSH—TURBO SPEED!

Didi slammed the levers forward and stomped on the brake. Robo-Dodo landed gracefully in front of the central library.

Actually, it was more like the RUINS of the central library! Books and bricks were scattered everywhere.

In the middle of it all was the Queen on her scooter, with the chicks riding on the back.

"The monster is headed for the art museum!" she yelled through the phone.

"Oh no!" I yelled back. "Not the art museum where they have the famous *Mona Spaghetti* painting!"

"Yes! That art museum! Now, quick! Follow me!"

The Queen revved her engine and zoomed down the street. I couldn't hear them, but I could plainly see that the baby chicks were screaming "UH-OH" at the top of their tiny lungs. (And also possibly pooping on the scooter seat.)

Didi worked the levers, and Robo-Dodo zoomed after them at top speed.

Chapter 12

The monster had ripped the roof off the art museum and was gulping down priceless works of art!

"Should I blast it with my la-ser beams?" asked Robo-Dodo.

"Of course not!" I yelled. "What are you telling me with the laser beams! We are cookie makers, not eel blasters!"

Chapter 12

The monster had ripped the roof off the art museum and was gulping down priceless works of art!

"Should I blast it with my la-ser beams?" asked Robo-Dodo.

"Of course not!" I yelled. "What are you telling me with the laser beams! We are cookie makers, not eel blasters!"

"Yes, Didi, I see it," I said. "But I am afraid to push it."

"But that button is part of my daring plan!"

"I know," I said. "That's why I'm afraid to push it!"

"Well, which is scarier: the button or THAT?"

She pointed out the window. The giant eel monster was right in front of us!

"THAT!" I answered. I held one wing over the big scary button, ready to push when we got to that part of the plan . . . but I was hoping we wouldn't get to that part of the plan.

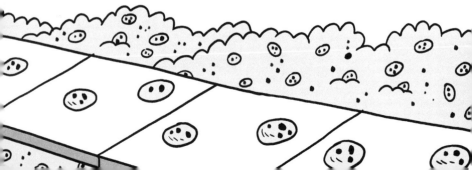

"How are those cookies coming?" Didi yelled over her shoulder.

"The first batch of fif-ty thou-sand cookies is rea-dy," answered Robo-Dodo.

"Great! Load them onto the cookie conveyor belt and start baking more!" she ordered. "Koko, do you see that big button that says 'DEFINITELY DON'T PUSH THIS BUTTON? NO KIDDING! SERIOUSLY! THE OTHER ONE WASN'T THAT BIG A DEAL, BUT THIS ONE WILL CAUSE COMPLETE COOKIE CHAOS!'?"

"The monster is headed for the art museum!" she yelled through the phone.

"Oh no!" I yelled back. "Not the art museum where they have the famous *Mona Spaghetti* painting!"

"Yes! That art museum! Now, quick! Follow me!"

The Queen revved her engine and zoomed down the street. I couldn't hear them, but I could plainly see that the baby chicks were screaming "UH-OH" at the top of their tiny lungs. (And also possibly pooping on the scooter seat.)

Didi worked the levers, and Robo-Dodo zoomed after them at top speed.

"Gee," said Robo-Dodo. "I have learned an im-por-tant les-son to-day. May-be the real mon-ster is—"

"Learn your lesson later," interrupted Didi. "First, we've got an eel to stuff! Look!"

The eel was opening its mouth really wide! It looked like it would eat the entire museum gift shop in one gigantic bite!

"NOOOOO! NOT THE GIFT SHOP!" yelled Didi. "PUSH THE BUTTON, KOKO!"

I pushed the button.

Deep within Robo-Dodo, powerful engines roared to life. The entire walking robotic cookie factory began to shake.

The conveyor belt began spinning at 392 miles per hour!

The giant beak opened!

Dozens, hundreds, thousands of cookies shot out of the beak and right into the gaping mouth of the giant eel monster!

"Yum!" said the eel as it swallowed them all.

The cookies kept flying and the monster kept eating and eating.

"Can't . . . keep . . . up . . . much . . . lon-ger . . ." groaned Robo-Dodo.

"Hang in there!" yelled Didi.

"More! More!" said the giant eel monster.

"Don't talk with your mouth full!" yelled the Queen.

"Sorry," said the giant eel monster with its mouth full. "It's just that these cookies are SO good! Just like my mom used to make!"

The cookies were still pouring out and the eel hadn't missed one yet.

"Mmm . . . I'm starting to feel full," the giant eel moaned.

"Just a little more!" yelled Didi.

A screen started blinking. "ALERT: COOKIE LEVEL LOW!"

"Robo-Dodo! Can you give us any more?"

"One . . . last . . . batch . . ." wheezed Robo-Dodo. One thousand more cookies dropped onto the conveyor belt and were shot into the eel's mouth.

"WONDERFUL!" slobbered the monster. "I've almost had all I can eat. Maybe just one more?"

"No . . . more . . ." said Robo-Dodo. It shuddered and stumbled. "Out of fuel . . . Out of coo-kies . . . Out of biz-ness . . ."

"The daring plan just changed!" yelled Didi. "Jump! This robot is about to crash!"

We jumped out of the hole in the roof and skated down the beak, just as Robo-Dodo began to tip backward.

"Dim-ple-hammmmmmmm . . ." Robo-Dodo groaned as it toppled over, directly onto the museum gift shop!

Then came the horrible sounds of glass breaking, bricks crumbling, and thousands of coffee mugs smashing into bits.

And then . . . silence. Robo-Dodo didn't move.

"The mighty metal dodo is no more," said the Queen.

"No more?" asked the giant eel monster. "You mean no more cookies? But I thought it was all-you-can-eat? I've got room for one more!"

"Uh . . . sorry," said Didi.

"This is an outrage!" yelled the giant eel. "I'm going to give this place ZERO STARS on MonsterBook and I'm NEVER coming back again!"

It slithered back into the sea and never came back again.

"You did it, Didi!" I yelled. "You saved the city."

Didi was looking at the remains of the art museum gift shop. Robo-Dodo was lying on a heap of torn tote bags and broken coffee mugs.

"Yes," said Didi Dodo, "but at what cost? At what cost?"

Epilogue

ots of fire trucks, police cars, and TV news vans and one presidential limo showed up.

"What are you dumb birds doing here?" yelled the President. "This is a disaster area! Get outta here."

The Queen gave me and the baby chicks a ride back to the cookie shop, but Didi wouldn't come.

She said she had a plan, and I know better than to argue when she has a plan!

We got back to the shop, and it was just like we had left it: with dozens and dozens of unsold cookies!

"Uh-oh," said the baby chicks.

"What are we going to do with all these cookies?" asked the Queen.

"I don't know," I said sadly. "I just don't know."

Just then, Penguini came running in.

"Quick, my friends! Turn on your television! Didi is on the news!"

We turned on the TV and there she was, talking to famous TV newsperson Greta Von Hopinstop.

"As you can see," Greta was saying, "everyone is coming back to the city to see how much damage the sea monster has done."

The camera showed the bitten buildings, the busted library, the headless Cousin Yuk Yuk statue, and the smashed coffee mugs.

"Everyone is asking the same question," said Greta. "They are asking: How can we ever rebuild this city?"

"Don't worry, I have a plan," said Didi Dodo.

She waved her wing, she lifted her beak, and she sparkled her eyes right at the camera.

"And what is that plan?" asked Greta Von Hopinstop.

"I've repaired Robo-Dodo and repro-grammed it to make bricks to rebuild the city."

Robo-Dodo stomped onto the screen and opened its mouth, and a medium-size taco stand popped out. (Right on top of the President's new limo.)

"Hey!" neighed President Horse G. Horse angrily. "What do you think you—"

"That will be one pen-ny," said Robo-Dodo.

"Wow, what a bargain!" whinnied President Horse G. Horse happily. "Does anyone have a penny they can loan me?"

"Well," said the reporter, "it looks like everything is going to work out just fine. But where will everybody get their cookies?"

"At Ko-Ko Do-Do's Coo-kie Shop, of course," said Robo-Dodo. "He makes the best coo-kies in the ci-ty!"

Instantly, everyone in the city started running straight for my cookie shop! They all came barging in the door, yelling and hollering for cookies.

"Uh-oh," said the baby chicks.

"Keep calm," shouted the Queen. "We've got plenty of leftover cookies for everybody!"

Just then, Didi skated in.

"Here she is!" I shouted. "It's Didi Dodo, the daring dodo and future spy!"

The crowd started to cheer and then stopped cheering to jump out of the way, because Didi still doesn't know how to stop! She crashed right into the counter and double-chocolate chunk cookies flew everywhere . . . again!

"Sorry about the cookies," said Didi.

"Don't be worrying about it," I said. "Today, you SAVED the whole cookie shop!"

And I gave her a free cookie.

TOM ANGLEBERGER is the *New York Times* bestselling author of the Origami Yoda series, as well as many other books for kids. He created Koko Dodo with his wife, Cece Bell, for the Inspector Flytrap series. When that series ended, he still wanted to send Koko on some bigger adventures . . . whether Koko wanted to go or not! Visit Tom at origamiyoda.com.

ABOUT THE ILLUSTRATOR

JARED CHAPMAN is the author-illustrator of the bestselling *Vegetables in Underwear*, as well as *Fruits in Suits* and *Pirate, Viking & Scientist*. He lives in Texas. Find out more about Jared at jaredchapman.com.